Lucy's Christmas

WRITTEN BY

Donald Hall

ILLUSTRATED BY

Michael McCurdy

Browndeer Press

Harcourt Brace & Company

SAN DIEGO   NEW YORK   LONDON

Requests for permission to make copies of any part of
the work should be mailed to: Permissions Department,
Harcourt Brace & Company, 6277 Sea Harbor Drive, Orlando, Florida 32887-6777.

Library of Congress Cataloging-in-Publication Data
Hall, Donald, 1928–
Lucy's Christmas/by Donald Hall; illustrated by
Michael McCurdy. — 1st ed.
p.   cm.
"Browndeer Press."
Summary: In the fall of 1909, Lucy gets an early start on making Christmas
presents for her family and friends, which they will open at the church's Christmas program.
ISBN 0-15-276870-X
[1. Christmas — Fiction. 2. Gifts — Fiction. 3. United States —
Social life and customs — 1865–1918 — Fiction.]
I. McCurdy, Michael, ill. II. Title.
PZ7.H14115Lu   1994
[E] — dc20   92-46292

First edition   A B C D E

Printed in Singapore

The illustrations in this book were done in colored scratchboard on Rising Photolene paper.
The display type was set in Nicholas Cochin by Thompson Type, San Diego, California.
The text type was set in Cloister by Thompson Type, San Diego, California.
Color separations were made by Bright Arts, Ltd., Singapore.
Printed and bound by Tien Wah Press, Singapore
Production supervision by Warren Wallerstein and David Hough
Designed by Trina Stahl

For Emily and Ariana
— D. H.

For Jane Clausen, my godchild
— M. M.

Late in August a branch of the sugar maple turned red, which made Lucy think of autumn and winter.

Lucy Wells liked planning ahead.

Even though it was far off, she thought about Christmas at the South Danbury Church, where all the families in the village opened their presents together.

So she started making Christmas presents.

She sewed scraps of velvet, left over from a dress her mother made, into a little bag. Then she stuffed it with bits of sheep's wool that her father sheared last April and that she had saved in the box under her bed.

Oil in the sheep's wool would keep pins and needles from rusting.

She sewed the pincushion shut and packed it away in her secret box to give to her mother for Christmas.

On cool mornings Lucy played with her little sister, Caroline, beside the old kitchen stove, where it was warm.

Early last month her mother and father had looked through the Sears catalogue to find a new stove.

They liked to plan ahead, too.

Caroline had pointed to a picture of a beautiful range — but it was too big for their kitchen.

All of them liked a pretty stove — but it was too small.

Then Lucy pointed to a picture of the latest Glenwood Kitchen Range.

It was just the right size.

Everybody agreed with Lucy's choice, and they mailed their order to Sears Roebuck in Chicago.

One morning in September a frost turned all the trees yellow and red. School started.

Lucy spent her days again at Eagle Pond School with her best friend, Rebecca Smart, with her cousin Charley Huntoon, and with all the other children.

One Saturday Lucy shut herself into her room. She drew a lady's face at the top of a wooden clothespin. Using scraps from her box, she made the doll a pretty dress and a hat with a yellow feather from a baby chick that she saved from when she watered the chickens last summer.

Caroline would have a clothespin doll for Christmas.

The third week of school, Lucy told her mother, "We're writing with steel pens now. We dip them into inkwells on our own desks!"

"Sometimes do you drip ink on the paper by mistake?" asked Lucy's mother.

Lucy said that sometimes *Rebecca* dripped a little drop.

"Let me show you something," said her mother.

Later that evening Lucy cut pieces of flannel, left over from making nightgowns, into circles of different colors and crimped them together to look like a big chrysanthemum with a button sewed in the middle.

Lucy had made a pen wiper for Rebecca for Christmas.

Nights were cold now. Leaves filled the yard. The kitchen range burned day and night. So did the stove in the living room, and at night Lucy and Caroline went to bed with hot water bottles.

Lucy's mother and father gathered apples and pressed them for vinegar.

Lucy's mother canned applesauce, covering the little stove with pots and pans.

"When will the Glenwood come?" Lucy asked every morning.

"They'll tell us down to the depot, when it gets here," said her mother.

"They'll tell us down to the depot, when it gets here," Caroline said to Lucy.

In November at Sunday school they rehearsed their parts for the church's Christmas program.

At home their mothers made them costumes that looked like the pictures in the Bible. Lucy thought about the baby in the manger, the star, and the wise men riding their camels.

Lucy also thought about big storybooks and dolls with eyes that opened and shut.

All year long her mother bought salt and coffee from the man in the Grand Union wagon, who stopped by the dooryard every Wednesday.

In summer the wagon had wheels. In winter it was a sleigh.

The Grand Union man gave her mother coupons for everything she bought, and a catalogue of Christmas presents she could order with the coupons.

Every autumn Lucy's mother mailed the coupons to Grand Union in Boston.

Every year at the church Christmas, Lucy's big presents were a new doll and a new storybook.

One rainy noontime Abel Baker, the Rural Free Delivery man, brought a post card from Railway Express. The new Glenwood Kitchen Range waited at the Danbury depot!

Lucy's father and the hired man carried the little old stove to a lean-to beside the sheep barn, just in case it ever came in handy. Then her father backed their horse, Riley, into the sledge.

"Do you want to come?" said Lucy's father.

Lucy and Caroline squeezed into the front seat, and they slid over rolled snow to the railroad station.

They came back with a huge wooden packing case.

It took two hours to put the new stove together. The kitchen was cold before they fixed the new chimney pipe and laid the fire.

The beautiful new Glenwood was huge, black, and cast-iron, with bright nickel trim. It had its own reservoir, where the water stayed warm all day but never boiled away. It had levers all over, to control the heat so that everything cooked at the right temperature.

It was Queen of the Kitchen!

All the neighbors dropped by, sleighs in the dooryard, to see the new stove.

"My goodness!" the neighbors said. "Did you ever see such a stove?"

"What a wonder!"

While she was at school Lucy missed the new Glenwood. She talked about it in recess. When she came home she sat in front of it, gazing.

"What a wonder!" said Lucy. "Did you ever see such a stove?"

When her mother baked a cake, the thermometer built into the iron door registered 350 degrees.

Lucy's mother studied how to cook in the modern way — baking bread, simmering soup, cooking chicken fricassee, boiling New England dinner, and stirring up red flannel hash.

Lucy asked, "Will you teach me how to cook?"

"We can start," said her mother.

She showed Lucy how to open the oven with the foot pedal and set bread inside without touching the iron.

She showed her how to set a skillet where the stove was hottest, to melt lard for doughnuts. Caroline stood watching.

"You'll learn next year," said Lucy.

Then Lucy helped Caroline make Christmas presents for their mother and father.

At Henry's store they bought tiny sticky-backed calendars, three for a nickel. They also bought two yards of pink netting and strips of colored paper with stickum at one end. From the paper strips, the girls glued red and green chains to hang from wall to wall across the church. Then Lucy helped Caroline draw cat pictures on two pieces of white cardboard and stick the calendars underneath them.

"Imagine!" said Lucy to Caroline. "It's going to be 1910!"

Lucy counted out fifty-two pieces of tissue paper, punched holes in a corner, and tied them between cardboard covers with red yarn. On the front she drew the stick figure of a little boy. Then she wrote a title for her tissue paper book: *Little Shaver.*

It was a Christmas present for her father — a book of tissues to wipe his straight razor on, when he shaved Sunday mornings sitting on the set tub, using the mirror under the twenty-four-hour clock.

Finally, school was out for Christmas.

The day before the church's Christmas program, Lucy and Caroline popped popcorn — their father had grown it all summer by the barn — on the new Glenwood. Then Lucy and Caroline and their mother made popcorn bags out of the pink netting from Henry's store. In each bag they put two pieces of ribbon candy and a whole handful of popcorn. It took them all day.

The next day the girls were up early. Their father sat on the set tub shaving, even though it wasn't Sunday. The girls wrapped their presents. Lucy wondered what Caroline's present for *her* was, because Caroline giggled so much.

Their father milked the cows.

Their mother baked beans and brown bread in the Glenwood.

When their father stopped by the door with Riley and the sleigh, the girls packed their presents and costumes behind the seat. Riley pulled them quickly over the slick snow. They passed Rebecca's farm and their cousin Charley's.

When Lucy and Caroline walked into the South Danbury Christian Church, it was alight with bright colors. The Christmas tree was covered with popcorn strings and pink bags of candy and popcorn, chains of bright paper festooned overhead from wall to wall, where every oil lamp blazed high, and the big light glowed in the center of the ceiling.

Lucy and Caroline put their packages under the tree, to one side of the pulpit, and sat up front with the other children from Sunday school.

Ella Downes, who was only four, led the church in the Lord's Prayer. Martha Morrill and Edna Sleeper and Lucille Sanborn sang "Silent Night" while David Cilley played the piano.

Then everybody sang "O Come, All Ye Faithful" and "O Little Town of Bethlehem."

Lucy's cousin Charley Huntoon played the accordion. Clara Braley, who was eleven, recited "'Twas the night before Christmas" all the way through without a mistake. Caroline and the other five year olds, Olan Clark and Artelia Elkins and Allison Fifield, said a poem about cows and sheep in the manger.

Then everybody sang "It Came upon a Midnight Clear" and "We Three Kings of Orient Are."

Then the children ducked into the church's hallway and tugged their costumes over their regular clothes. Lucy stood up with Rebecca and read the Christmas story from the Scriptures. While they read, the rest of Sunday school acted the story in pantomime.

Caroline was a Shepherd. Charley's younger brother, Clarence, was the Star.

Lucy read, "And when they saw the star, they rejoiced with exceeding great joy."

Rebecca read, "And the shepherds returned, glorifying and praising God for all the things that they had seen and heard."

Then it was time for presents.

Martha and Edna and Lucille delivered red and green packages to everybody in church. Lucy and Caroline looked at their new storybooks.

Caroline hugged a new doll with eyes that opened and shut.

Lucy had a pretty little doll from her aunt Susan and a doll's cradle from her big cousin Charley. He made it himself out of scraps from his father's sawmill. Rebecca gave her a toy village she made by cutting pictures out of magazines and pasting them to cardboard.

Rebecca loved her flower pen wiper.

Lucy also had a doll's nightgown, a board game called Railroad, and a new set of dominoes. Caroline had tiddlywinks and tiny doll's booties and a map of the United States that was a puzzle because the states were separate pieces.

She put the doll's booties on the clothespin doll from Lucy.

Lucy's next-to-last present was from Caroline — and it was a calendar pasted under a cat picture drawn on cardboard! Lucy remembered: the calendars were *three* for a nickel.

Lucy waited for another package, shaped like a doll with eyes that opened and shut, but it didn't come.

She lifted her last present, from her mother and father. It was a small package, but it was heavy. She couldn't imagine what it could be.

It was a tiny cast-iron Glenwood Kitchen Range — with a tiny oven door that opened and shut, with tiny lids and tiny lifters the right size for her tiny doll's skillet and kettle — and with its own tiny reservoir for hot water.

"You can practice cooking on it," said Lucy's mother.

"You can practice on it, too," said Lucy to Caroline, "while I'm at school."

When they tucked into the sleigh for the ride home, Caroline put her
clothespin doll in the arms of her big doll with eyes that opened and shut and
cuddled them both. Lucy cuddled her storybook in one arm and her stove
in the other.

They both fell asleep as they slipped home, warm under woolen blankets
with Riley pulling the sleigh over snow through the darkness under a million stars.

AFTERWORD

A long time ago my mother, Lucy, and her sister Caroline lived in a New Hampshire farmhouse with their father and mother, who milked cows and raised sheep. As I grew up my mother told me stories of her childhood — about making presents for the Christmas celebration at the church and about the day a new wood-burning range arrived at the farm.

Now ninety years old, my mother lives in Connecticut in the house where my family moved in 1936. My wife and I live in the New Hampshire farmhouse where she was born, and once a month we drive to see her — to run errands, to visit, and to reminisce about the past. The Glenwood range that my mother remembers still lords it over the kitchen. And in the back chamber, above our dining room, among broken rocking chairs and doll's furniture, we keep the toy cast-iron range that Lucy received at the South Danbury Church Christmas when she was a girl.

—D. H.